Weekly Reader Children's Book Club presents

PETUNIA, BEWARE!

by Roger Duvoisin

New York • Alfred A. Knopf

This book is a presentation of Weekly Reader Books.
Weekly Reader Books offers book clubs for children from preschool through high school.
For further information write to: **Weekly Reader Books,** 4343 Equity Drive, Columbus, Ohio 43228.

A Borzoi book published by arrangement with Alfred A. Knoff, Inc.
Weekly Reader™ is a trademark of Field Publications.

This title was originally catalogued by the Library of Congress as follows:

E-DUV   Duvoisin, Roger.   Petunia, beware! Illus. by the author.

Summary: The silly goose, Petunia, investigates the grass on the other side of the fence.

1. Geese—Stories   I. Title

L.C. Catalog Card number: 58-9938   ISBN: 0-394-90867-8 (Lib. ed.)

Petunia never ate what she had in her own dish.

Hoping for a better treat, she always ate from her friends' dishes.

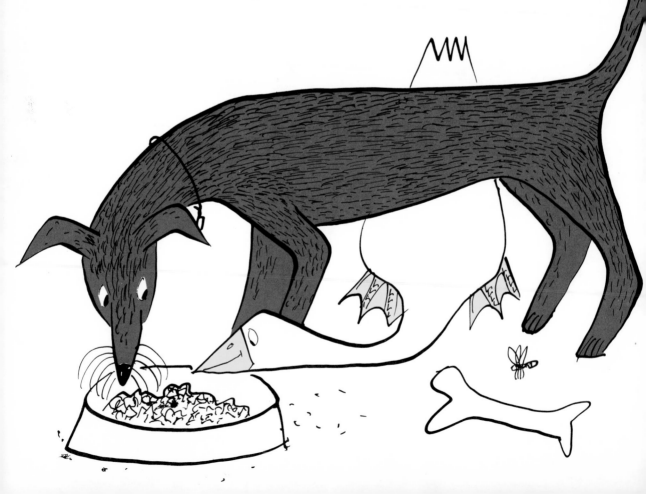

She *never* touched the grass on her side of the fence, but *always* clipped what she could from the neighbor's meadow. Foolish Petunia never liked what was in her own yard. She wanted only what she didn't have.

"Ah," she sighed, looking through the fence at the grassy hills across the stream. "Think of the fine meals I am missing every day. How green is the grass on Windy Hill.

"Noisy," she said to the dog, "let's leave our yard and taste the wonderful green grass in the meadow beyond the fence."

"I never eat grass," yawned Noisy, "which shouldn't stop you from going alone. *BUT* beware of the wild animals!"

Foolish Petunia flicked her wing feathers and walked
out into the wild, wide, greener world.

She plucked some grass from the neighbor's meadow.
BUT

The grass *wasn't* a bit greener.
It *wasn't* a bit tastier.
IT WAS THE SAME GRASS!

"Well," she said, "I'll walk on further."

"Good morning, Petunia," said the rabbit, popping out from under a stump. "Where are you going?"

"Good morning, Mr. Rabbit," said Petunia. "I am going to the next meadow to eat the greener, tastier grass under the old oak tree."

"Beware of the cruel weasel, Petunia. He poked his nose under my stump this very morning and gave me such a fright."

Petunia pulled a beakful of grass from under the old oak tree. *BUT*

The grass *wasn't* a bit greener.
It *wasn't* a bit tastier.
IT WAS THE SAME GRASS!

"Well," she said, "let's walk further."

"Good morning, Petunia," said the woodchuck, peering out of his hole. "Where are you going?"

"Good morning, Mr. Woodchuck. I am going to that meadow beyond the dogwoods to eat the greener, tastier grass."

"Beware of the fox, Petunia. I smelled his tracks past the stone fence this very dawn. The thief."

Petunia pulled a few blades of grass from the meadow
beyond the dogwoods. *BUT*

The grass *wasn't* a bit greener.
It *wasn't* a bit tastier.
IT WAS THE SAME GRASS!

"Well," she said, "I'll just have to walk further."

"Good morning, Petunia," chattered the chipmunk, sitting up straight on a maple stump. "Where are you going?"

"Good morning, Mr. Chipmunk. I am going to that meadow at the edge of the brook to eat the greener, tastier grass."

"Beware of the fierce old raccoon, Petunia. He peeped into my hole this very morning, but my hole is too small for his claws."

When she reached the meadow at the edge of the brook, Petunia could hardly believe that

The grass *wasn't* a bit greener.
It *wasn't* a bit tastier.
IT WAS THE SAME GRASS!

"Well," she said, "let's walk further."

"Good morning, Petunia," said the deer, browsing at the edge of the wood. "Where are you going?"

"Good morning, Mr. Deer. I am going to the meadow on top of Windy Hill to eat the greener, tastier grass."

"Beware of the bobcat, Petunia. It slunk past the deer-crossing early this morning."

When Petunia reached the top of Windy Hill she could hardly believe it. *BUT*

The grass was not green.
It was not tasty.
IT WAS DRY GRASS.

"Well," she said, looking down the hill at her farm below, "how VERY GREEN the grass looks in the meadow near the barn. I never thought my own meadow looked so green and tasty. Well, let's walk back."

"Why hurry, Petunia?" said a little voice behind her.
"You are the loveliest, fattest goose I have ever seen.
And I am so hungry."

IT WAS THE CRUEL WEASEL!

"Yes, do stay, Petunia," said a rasping voice behind a bush. "Do not listen to the kind words of our friend. The weasel will not touch one of your feathers while I am with you."

IT WAS THE FOX!

"Yes, don't leave quite yet, Petunia," said a silky voice from the long grass. "Do not fear Weasel and Fox while I am here."

IT WAS THE FIERCE, OLD RACCOON!

"Yes, do wait a while, Petunia," said a soft, purring voice from a clump of birches. Weasel, Fox, and Raccoon will not harm you while I am protecting you."

IT WAS THE BOBCAT!

Petunia was so cold with fear that she could not move.
She closed her eyes and thought of her farm in the lovely
green valley.

The four greedy rascals leaped forward all together.
They crashed into a hissing, yowling, clawing, biting
jumble. The jumble looked like a four-headed dragon
with sixteen legs and four tails. Petunia gathered all her

strength and rushed down the hill, half running, half sliding (she was too heavy to fly well). She had reached the meadow at the edge of the brook when her enemies saw that she was gone.

They ran and tumbled down the hill after her. Over the brook, past the dogwood trees, and through the meadow with the old oak tree they ran.

But they were too LATE.

As Petunia, honking faintly, reached the neighbor's meadow, Noisy the dog dashed out barking LOUDLY, and put Weasel, Fox, Raccoon, and Bobcat to flight.

After Petunia had thanked Noisy, she recovere
enough to pull a few blades of grass from her ow
meadow — AND —

IT WAS THE BEST GRASS
THAT SHE HAD
EVER TASTED